The Butterfly Robber

Written by Jill Eggleton
Illustrated by Richard Hoit

There were butterflies
everywhere in Butterfly Park.
They were all the colors
of the rainbow.
They danced in the sky
with the sun on their wings.

People loved the butterflies
at Butterfly Park.

But one day,
Boris came to the park.
He had a big sack
and a big net.
He was a butterfly robber.

When no one was looking,
he got out his net and
whooooosh,
all the butterflies
were gone from the sky.

Boris took the butterflies
to a cave.
He put them inside and
shut the rock door.

"I am going to have
all the butterflies
for myself," he said.
"I will catch every butterfly.
No one will see them but me!"

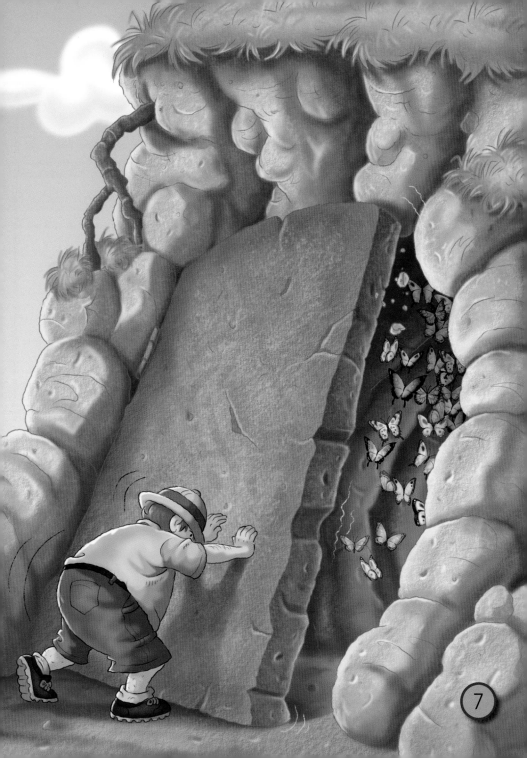

The people at the park
didn't know where
the butterflies had gone.
They looked everywhere.
They looked every day,
but they couldn't find them.

"The butterflies made us happy,"
they said.
"Now they are all gone."

Closed
No More
Butterflies

Boris went to his cave.
"I will watch the butterflies
dance now," he said.

But when Boris looked
in the cave, the butterflies
were lying on the ground,
and they were
all white!

"Oh, no!" said Boris.
"The butterflies are sick."

Boris put the butterflies
in his net and took them
out of the cave.

"I can't keep you for myself,"
he said.
"You must make
everyone happy.
You must dance in the sky
with the sun on your wings."

And he let the butterflies go.

The butterflies went
back to the park.
The colors came into
their wings again.
They danced in the sky and
the people were happy.

But now every butterfly
has a little white spot.
And no one knows why.
No one but Boris!

A Story Sequence

1

2

3

4

Guide Notes

Title: **The Butterfly Robber**
Stage: Early (4) – Green

Genre: Fiction
Approach: Guided Reading
Processes: Thinking Critically, Exploring Language, Processing Information
Written and Visual Focus: Story Sequence
Word Count: 279

THINKING CRITICALLY
(sample questions)
- What do you think this story could be about? Look at the title and discuss.
- Look at the cover. What do you think the butterfly robber is going to do?
- Look at pages 2 and 3. Why do you think the people like the butterflies?
- Look at pages 4 and 5. Why do you think the butterflies were not able to escape from Boris's net?
- Look at pages 6 and 7. Why do you think Boris wanted the butterflies all for himself?
- Look at pages 8 and 9. What else do you think the people could do to find the butterflies?
- Look at pages 10 and 11. Why do you think the butterflies are sick? Why do you think the butterflies have turned white?
- Look at page 14. Why do you think the butterflies have a white spot on them now?

EXPLORING LANGUAGE

Terminology
Title, cover, illustrations, author, illustrator

Vocabulary
Interest words: rainbow, park, cave, robber, people
High-frequency words: everywhere, know, catch
Positional words: in, inside, on, out, into
Compound words: butterfly, butterflies, rainbow, myself, inside, everywhere, everyone

Print Conventions
Capital letter for sentence beginnings and names (**B**utterfly **P**ark, **B**oris), periods, commas, exclamation marks, quotation marks